Dayboil

Dayboil

A PLAY BY

SHARON KING-CAMPBELL

BREAKWATER BOOKS
P.O. Box 2188, St. John's, NL, Canada, A1C 6E6
WWW.BREAKWATERBOOKS.COM

A CIP catalogue record for this book is available from Library and
Archives Canada.

ISBN 9781778530128 (softcover)

© 2024 Sharon King-Campbell

Cover illustration: Brooklyn Mitchell, Gair Designs Inc.

We acknowledge the support of the Canada Council for the Arts.

We acknowledge the financial support of the Government of Canada
through the Department of Heritage and the Government of
Newfoundland and Labrador through the Department of Tourism,
Culture, Arts and Recreation for our publishing activities.

PRINTED AND BOUND IN CANADA.

Canada Council   Conseil des Art   Canada   Newfoundland
for the Arts   du Canada   Labrador

Breakwater Books is committed to choosing papers and materials for
our books that help to protect our environment. To this end, this book
is printed on a recycled paper and other sources that are certified by the
Forest Stewardship Council®.

Dayboil was first performed at Ship's Company Theatre in Parrsboro, Nova Scotia on July 27, 2022, under the artistic direction of Richie Wilcox, with the following team:

CAST

Kathy	*Stephanie MacDonald*
Patricia	*Karen Bassett*
Christine	*Sharleen Kalayil*
Eunice	*Sherry Smith*
Jennifer	*Riley McGill*
Kevin	*Taylor Olson*

CREATIVE TEAM AND CREW

Director	*Samantha Wilson*
Set Design	*Katrin Whitehead*
Costume Design	*Avery Morris*
Sound Design	*Aaron Collier*
Lighting Design	*Alison Crosby*
Stage Manager	*Patricia Vinluan*
Assistant Stage Manager	*Virg Iredale*
Technical Director	*Scott Miller*
Crew	*Alexa Kirste*
House Technician	*Gina Woodward*
Carpentry	*Andrew Kerr*

Dayboil was developed in part at the Playwrights Atlantic Resource Centre Playwright's Retreat.

Foreword

I was first introduced to the script of *Dayboil* through an annual retreat put on by Playwrights Atlantic Resource Centre (PARC) in 2019. I was sitting in an intimate classroom at Mount Allison University with ten or so audience members forming an outer circle, looking in on the actors seated at a table in the middle of the room. I laughed a lot. I cried more.

The most prevailing thing I felt was connection. The small-town characters were so relatable. The gender dynamics, and the critiques of those assigned roles, hit hard. The struggling mental health and addiction issues were all too real. Most of all, the script showed humour, anger, and sadness in the face of death. Grief wasn't boxed in as being only sentimental and romantic. *Dayboil* shows messy grief. It's brutally honest. And those truths punch you in the gut.

This play was originally titled *A Good Cup of Tea Won't Fix It*, and I knew it had to be produced as soon as I heard it. I wanted to be a part of that journey.

When I became the artistic director of Ship's Company Theatre in 2019, I jumped at the opportunity to bring that dream to fruition. Sharon King-Campbell had known of my love of the play from that first read, and thankfully gave Ship's and myself the green light to produce the world premiere production of *Dayboil* in the summer of 2021.

Ship's Company is located in a very rural part of Nova Scotia that has a high poverty rate, mental health and addiction issues, and a high suicide rate. And yet, who really talks about these things in the open? When do we actually address the heart-wrenching problems that are in front of us day to day? *Dayboil* served as a cathartic way in for audiences. It served as a catalyst for conversation. It gave people a chance to connect, especially on the tough stuff of life.

The production was celebrated by the Nova Scotia theatre community, winning six of the top Robert Merritt Awards that year, including Outstanding Production. But the biggest success was how much the audiences embraced the show. People assume we all want comedies and fluffy escapism entertainment. *Dayboil* was the antidote we were all craving and didn't even know we needed.

I'm forever grateful to Sharon for letting me have a hand in the development of this piece. I'm even more thankful that she sat down one day and chose to write about these topics, through these characters, within this world.

Unlike a good cup of tea, I believe telling stories like this *can* fix things.

— *Richie Wilcox*

CHARACTERS

KATHY   *A paramedic. Late 30s.*

PATRICIA   *Kathy's sister, full-time homemaker.*
Early 40s.

CHRISTINE   *Patricia's best friend, works at the café.*
Early 40s.

EUNICE   *Kathy and Patricia's childhood neighbour,*
generally a motherly figure. 60s.

JENNIFER   *Staying with her grandparents for the*
summer and working at the café. 17.

KEVIN   *Kathy's husband, technician with the cable*
company. Late 30s.

SETTING

Kathy and Kevin's kitchen in a small town in
Newfoundland and Labrador. The side door leads directly
into the kitchen. There is another door at the front of the
house, but it is never used.

SCENE I

Lights up.

KATHY slams in through the side entrance, holding a muffin tin and, on top of it, a grocery store box of twelve muffins in one hand, and the pot from a coffee maker, full to the brim, in the other. She shoves the door closed with her bum, kicks her boots off on the mat and crosses to the counter. She puts down everything and tries to trade out the empty pot in her coffee maker for the full one, only they are not the same size and the full one doesn't fit.

KATHY: Shit.

She pours the coffee from one pot to the other, opening the muffin box one-handed while she does it. When the smaller pot is full she puts it back in the coffee maker and flips it on, then gets a mug and pours in the remaining coffee. She takes a sip. The coffee maker gurgles, then starts to drip into the already-full pot.

KATHY: Oh shit shit shit!

KATHY pulls out the pot and moves the whole unit to the sink. She leaves it there to pour coffee directly onto the burner, sputtering and steaming. While it does its thing she puts the muffins in a muffin tin, throws the tin into

*the oven and turns it on. She takes the now-finished
coffee maker out of the sink, turns it off, wets a cloth,
wipes the burner and all sides of the coffee maker, turns
it back on, puts the full pot back, and takes a sip of her
coffee. She takes off her coat and hangs it by the door.*

Enter PATRICIA. *She comes in without knocking, almost
banging into* KATHY *in the process. The women share
an uncomfortable moment as* KATHY *navigates her way
around* PATRICIA *and back into the kitchen.* PATRICIA
tidies KATHY*'s boots to one side, takes off her own coat
and boots.* KATHY *hastily stashes the muffin box in a
cupboard, then busies herself with cleaning out the sink.*
PATRICIA *helps herself to a mug for coffee, peeks into the
oven. She glances back at* KATHY.

PATRICIA: Hmm.

PATRICIA *turns down the temperature and brings* KATHY
the kettle. KATHY *fills it and puts it on the stove to boil.*
PATRICIA *sits at the table, pulls a newspaper out of her
purse and reads.*

Enter EUNICE.

EUNICE: Good morning, dears!

KATHY: Good morning, Eunice. How are you this week?

EUNICE: Oh, glad to be out of the house, I'll say that.
I feel like I've been trapped inside for days! Not even good
enough weather to hang out clothes!

PATRICIA: No, not a bit of good weather all week. My boys
are going squirrelly. Cabin fever, right?

EUNICE: Yes, that's it, that's what it is. Wait now until winter comes, and see how cabin feverish we get! How's Kathy today?

KATHY: Oh, fine.

There is a short pause while EUNICE *takes* KATHY *in.* KATHY *gives her a smile.*

PATRICIA: You're right, there, Eunice, it'll be ten times worse this winter. The boys are getting too big for the house, now. I got to send them to the basement just to feel like I have my kitchen back. They'll eat anything. I swear, if we ran out of bread they'd pull down the cupboard doors to make sandwiches!

EUNICE: Good to see young men eat, though, isn't it?

PATRICIA: It is that, yeah.

Enter CHRISTINE, *with a box under one arm. She is wearing scrubs under her coat.*

CHRISTINE: Good morning, lovelies! Kathy, the house smells incredible, you've done it again. Now don't get offended, but I managed to liberate these cookies from the café to go with our tea.

KATHY, *remembering, pulls the muffins out of the oven and lays them on the counter. Meanwhile:*

EUNICE: Christine, you can't go stealing from work!

PATRICIA: She's only teasing, Eunice. I'd say she paid full price for each cookie, didn't you Chris?

CHRISTINE: Don't worry, Eunice, I'm not as delinquent as I let on. I gets a discount though.

PATRICIA: And how's the tea room this morning?

CHRISTINE: Oh, the fellers are in fine form, gabbing on with their nonsense. Politics this and economy that, all the bad news in the world. I don't let Cameron go on about that stuff at home, so when he gets together with that crowd he lets it all fly. Sure I don't think he even noticed me leaving.

KATHY: I'm sure he did, Chris.

CHRISTINE: No girl, I'd say not. There's a new girl down there working, she's Mary's great-niece, seventeen years old. Not very many of them can see much besides her when she's serving 'em.

PATRICIA: No, I'd say they can't. I wouldn't say Pete could do it.

CHRISTINE: Oh, Pete's no worse than the rest of 'em. Maddie's girl. Remember Madeleine Hollett?

PATRICIA: Oh my Lord. How could I forget?

CHRISTINE: Well this girl's the spit out of Maddie's mouth, I can tell you. Looks the same, acts the same. All hips and eyelashes.

PATRICIA: Christ. No wonder the boys are all wrapped up in her.

EUNICE: Who's this?

PATRICIA: She was in our class. You remember her, Eun— Clar and Tasha's youngest.

CHRISTINE: Spoilt rotten too. Used to getting her way.

EUNICE: Oh yes. Pretty girl. Whatever happened to her?

PATRICIA: Dunno. She took off to the mainland right after school.

CHRISTINE: And thank God for that, too.

> *PATRICIA and* CHRISTINE *laugh.* KATHY *gets out two more mugs for* EUNICE *and* CHRISTINE *and lays them on the table with milk and sugar.*

CHRISTINE: I didn't see Kevin down to the café today, Kathy.

KATHY: Yeah . . . he's working this morning.

EUNICE: Imagine that, a man at work! A rare sight this time of year.

PATRICIA: If they were working, of course, Christine would have no chance to mock them to their faces, so there's that.

CHRISTINE: Yes, that's right, Pat, and my life would be the lesser for it.

PATRICIA: Silver linings.

> CHRISTINE *and* PATRICIA *share a laugh.* KATHY *has laid out the muffins on a plate and now brings them to the table.*

EUNICE: These muffins are just perfect, Kathy love, look how each one is just right. Symmetrical is the word. You've got a knack, my dear.

KATHY: Thanks, Eunice. Coffee?

EUNICE: I'll wait for tea, love.

PATRICIA: I'll have a top-up.

KATHY: Christine?

CHRISTINE: I shouldn't—I've already had my three cups this morning.

> KATHY *gets a glass of cold water for* CHRISTINE. *She does not bring the coffee to the table for* PATRICIA.

EUNICE: Jesus, Chris, three cups? The coffee down to Mary's isn't *that* good.

CHRISTINE: It's not the taste, Eun. I haven't had a wink since Jeremy left for his tour of duty.

EUNICE: But that was last month.

CHRISTINE: You don't have to tell me, girl, I'm ruined over it. Cameron's right proud of his son and sleeps like a baby, which is not fair. I'm proud too, don't think I'm not, but I can't get to sleep to save my life. I'm nodding off in the cheesecake every morning.

> PATRICIA *realizes her coffee is not coming and gets up to get it for herself.*

KATHY: Have you been up to see the doctor about it? You need to sleep.

CHRISTINE: Pfft. No girl, I'll manage now until I can get a handle on it.

EUNICE: That's right, my dear, a few sleepless nights is nothing to bother Dr. Shawarma with.

KATHY: Chandra.

EUNICE: Yes dear, that's what I meant, I can't ever get that right.

CHRISTINE: Pour me one too, would ya, Pat?

PATRICIA gets another mug from the cupboard and pours some coffee for CHRISTINE.

CHRISTINE: Anyway, he's only going to tell me what I already knows, I got to go to bed earlier, get some exercise during the day, drink less caffeine.

EUNICE: That's if you can understand him when /he talks, I can't—

KATHY: /There's decaf if //you want, Chris—

PATRICIA: //I got some melatonin down to the Shoppers, Chris, if you want to try it. Works wonders for me.

She delivers the coffee.

CHRISTINE: Yes girl, I might give it a shot, I'm at my wit's end.

CHRISTINE takes a sip of coffee. PATRICIA sits down. The kettle goes off. KATHY goes to make a pot of tea.

PATRICIA: Have you heard from Jeremy, though?

CHRISTINE: Oh yes, he calls every Sunday. He's doing good so far as he tells me.

EUNICE: I wish Amanda would call me every Sunday. How'd you get your youngsters to do that?

CHRISTINE: I didn't have to do very much with Jeremy. He raised himself, Mom always said.

PATRICIA: I suppose being on the other side of the world probably helps him feel a bit homesick, too.

CHRISTINE: Yes, I suppose you're right, there. Not very much of home over there.

EUNICE: No indeed.

> *General agreement. A pause.* EUNICE *pours herself a cup of tea.* KATHY *is scrubbing down the counters.*

EUNICE: Come sit down with us, love, you don't need to be at that right now.

CHRISTINE: Yeah, Kath, your kitchen is spotless anyway, I don't even know what you're cleaning.

PATRICIA: No kids, right? She's got different standards.

> KATHY *sits with the women for the first time this morning.*

KATHY: How's Amanda doing, Eunice?

EUNICE: Oh, good, girl, she got herself switched over to the day shifts now, so that's better, she can take the girls to school in the mornings, get her walk in, see the sun now and again. Avery's still away three weeks out of four, and that's hard on her, you know.

CHRISTINE: I don't suppose I'd mind too much if Cameron

was away three weeks out of four.

Laughter.

KATHY: She's liking Alberta?

EUNICE: Yes, I suppose she is. That's where the work is to, anyway.

PATRICIA: She's not homesick?

EUNICE: If she is, she doesn't show it. I wouldn't mind seeing a touch of homesickness in her.

KATHY: Is there much to do in Grande Prairie? Museums or movie theatres or anything?

CHRISTINE: You're not thinking of going up there, are you Kath?

KATHY: I don't know. Maybe.

CHRISTINE: You're not serious. You with a good job here.

PATRICIA: And Kevin, too.

The ladies all nod agreement, eyes on KATHY.

KATHY: I think it might be nice, you know, just to go somewhere else for a while. Check it out. They need paramedics everywhere.

EUNICE: And Kevin could find something to be at, I'm sure. He's a handy one.

Just the tiniest beat.

KATHY: Yes.

CHRISTINE: How is Kevin finding the new job?

KATHY: Oh . . . It's mostly driving around places. Going around answering calls and stuff. I don't know too much about it, really. He's late getting home a lot.

PATRICIA: Good thing you don't have any youngsters.

CHRISTINE: Down to the café the other day he was saying how stressful it is.

EUNICE: Is it? Poor dear. He works hard, that one.

KATHY: Well, it's hard to take it seriously when you've just done CPR. Or tried to keep a little kid calm while their parent is out cold, or had to pick up somebody's severed foot—

PATRICIA: Yuck, Kath, we're eating.

KATHY: —and he comes home all stressed from connecting cables to TVs all day. Like, nobody died, Kevin.

Beat. EUNICE *pats* KATHY's *hand.*

EUNICE: Now it's not that these cookies aren't excellent, but it's too bad you weren't able to thieve us a piece of your world-famous cheesecake, Chris.

CHRISTINE: Oh come on now, Eun.

EUNICE: Can't we be proud? Amanda found your picture in the paper there in Grande Prairie and mailed it to me.

PATRICIA: They're reading about your cheesecake all the way out in Vancouver.

CHRISTINE: Sure it's only Mom's recipe.

EUNICE: Makes you feel sorry for them folks up in Vancouver, don't it, that pay all that money just to rent a house and can't find any decent cheesecake. Got to read about it in the paper.

Laughter.

KATHY: Did you do the cookies, too? They're delicious.

CHRISTINE: No girl, that's Gert.

KATHY: Oh.

EUNICE: These muffins are lovely, too, Kath.

CHRISTINE: Yes, they are, too. You tell the hospital they better watch out or Mary'll scoop you up for her morning shift.

KATHY: They're really nothing.

EUNICE: Katherine Stoodley, don't be so down on yourself.

CHRISTINE: I likes the sugar you've put on the top. Feels right decadent.

KATHY: Thanks Chris.

EUNICE: How is the hospital, Kath?

KATHY: Oh, the same. I've mostly been doing calls the last few weeks. On the road a lot.

CHRISTINE: I heard that Jane Piercey went in with a pain in her belly and it came back it was cancer.

KATHY: You know I can't talk about that kind of stuff.

CHRISTINE: But was she there?

KATHY: Can't say.

CHRISTINE: Won't say.

PATRICIA: You're no fun, Kath.

KATHY: It's confidential, Pat. I can't say.

EUNICE: Ease up now, girls, you know she's not allowed. Sure just call Jane and ask her.

CHRISTINE: Yes now. "Janey, my dear, I heard from Mom's neighbour's daughter that you've got a belly full of cancer. Is it true?"

PATRICIA: Well, if she don't want people to know we can't make her tell. She *is* up to Shieldstown quite a bit now, though.

CHRISTINE: Yes, and to St. John's. She told me last week she was in seeing her new grandbaby and I didn't think nothing of it.

KATHY: She *does* have a new granddaughter. Fiona Louise.

PATRICIA: You can tell us that, when you weren't even there.

KATHY: She put it on Facebook, Pat.

EUNICE: Oh, I could never get the hang of that online business. Emails and that. /Amanda says she'd email me more than she can call but I just can't wrap my head around it.

KATHY: /And it's *because* I wasn't there that I can talk about it. I don't know about the baby because I was there when she was delivered, I know about the baby because I know her mother and she put pictures on Facebook.

EUNICE: Everything needs a password on the internet, right? /And I just can't keep them all straight.

KATHY: /Jane's granddaughter got nothing to do with my job, so I can talk about it, all right?

> KATHY *and* PATRICIA *stare each other down for the next four lines:*

CHRISTINE: I has a notepad by the computer where I writes all that down. Jeremy always told me it's no use having passwords if you're just going to have them written right next to the computer, but I can't keep it straight otherwise.

EUNICE: Chris, Amanda says there's like a phone that you can get for free through the internet, where I could see her face. Do you do that with Jeremy?

CHRISTINE: Oh yes, it's lovely. It chops up a bit and sometimes the picture isn't moving at the same time as the words, but I don't mind that if I can see with my own eyes he's safe and sound. It's complicated to get it started, though, he's got a list of instructions wrote out for me so I can figure it out.

EUNICE: Amanda'd probably have to write me a whole book. I finds it so confusing.

PATRICIA: I can send over one of the boys to set it up for you, Eunice.

EUNICE: Oh, would you? That'd be such a help.

PATRICIA: Of course. But you have to promise you won't judge me by the smell. Andrew hasn't got the hang of deodorant yet at all.

A general chuckle.

CHRISTINE: Oh, Pat, every boy goes through that. Sure Jeremy would just live in a heap of his own filth until I'd sneak in and do laundry for him. And then he'd be crooked with me for going into his room.

EUNICE: I only had Amanda. So the opposite problem, really, perfumes and scented soaps and the like. When she was still living at home you could barely walk past the bathroom without choking on the smell.

PATRICIA: You're lucky, you know, Kathy. Nobody stinking up your house.

CHRISTINE: If it's any consolation, Pat, as long as he smells that bad you won't have to worry about him with the girls!

Laughter.

KATHY: You know, the first time I was ever in Kevin's room we actually had to shove the dirty laundry off the bed for there to be room for us. And it smelled. And he wasn't even embarrassed.

PATRICIA: Didn't stop you though, did it?

KATHY: Barely any better now. Nothing like coming home from twelve hours at work, covered in vomit, or worse, and finding the clean laundry dumped out on the bed and nothing folded. And my husband having a beer in the living room at the end of *his* stressful day.

> EUNICE, CHRISTINE *and* PATRICIA *laugh.*

KATHY: Or he's out with Pete and I won't see him until the wee hours.

PATRICIA: I recall you asked me to send them out drinking together.

KATHY: Yes, a decade ago!

PATRICIA: Well, you can't blame me that it stuck!

> EUNICE *and* CHRISTINE *laugh.*

CHRISTINE: It's good for men to have some time away from us ladies, I think. Knows it's good to have time away from them!

EUNICE: Sure you sees their "man time" every day at the café, don'tcha Christine.

KATHY: They behave/ themselves at the café, though.

CHRISTINE: /Yes, and I wouldn't want to be along when they're drinking beer instead of coffee!

> *Laughter from all but* KATHY.

> *There is a frantic knock at the front door. The ladies exchange glances.* KATHY *gets up to answer it.*

> *As she does, the phone rings.*

KATHY: Pat.

PATRICIA *goes for the phone.* KATHY *opens the door, revealing* JENNIFER, *dressed in scrubs like* CHRISTINE.

JENNIFER: *(out of breath)* Are you . . . my aunt said . . . are you Katherine Stoodley?

KATHY: Yes. What's—

CHRISTINE: Jenny, what's the matter?

PATRICIA: *(into phone)* Stoodley residence, /this is Patricia.

JENNIFER: /I just heard a gunshot.

CHRISTINE: Come in girl, /are you sure?

PATRICIA: *(into phone)* /Slow down, //Gert, I can't make out—

JENNIFER: //Dead sure.

CHRISTINE: Where were you?

JENNIFER: Just outside the café, I just finished my shift.

CHRISTINE: Why didn't you go back inside?

JENNIFER: I ran! You run from guns.

PATRICIA: *(into phone)* Jesus Christ.

JENNIFER: I went to the house but I forgot my keys at work. I can't get in.

KATHY: You're Mary's niece.

JENNIFER: Yeah. Jennifer.

CHRISTINE: Works up to the café.

KATHY: Where's Mary now?

JENNIFER: Went to Shieldstown.

KATHY: Stephen too?

JENNIFER: Yeah.

PATRICIA: *(into phone)* Okay yeah, I'll tell her. Thanks, Gert.

She hangs up.

KATHY: Call the police, Pat.

PATRICIA: They did that down to the café. Kathy, Gert says it was Bill and Donna's house.

KATHY: *(softly)* Oh fuck.

JENNIFER: Who's that?

CHRISTINE: Her in-laws.

KATHY: Jesus.

PATRICIA: The police are just getting there now, she said.

KATHY: Okay.

PATRICIA: You're going.

KATHY: Yeah.

EUNICE: I'll take her. Come on, my love. Coat. Chris can you—

All hands help KATHY *find boots and coat. Meanwhile:*

CHRISTINE: I parked on the road. You should be clear.

KATHY: Where's my purse?

EUNICE: Doesn't matter, love. Come on.

The two go out the side door. It closes. A long pause.
We hear the car pull out and away. Silence.

CHRISTINE: I'm going to put the kettle back on. Jenny, do you want some tea?

PATRICIA: Are you hungry?

JENNIFER: *(to* CHRISTINE*)* Okay.

PATRICIA: I'd say you're hungry.

JENNIFER: No.

PATRICIA: Well, I think I'll make some sandwiches, just in case.

CHRISTINE: Yes, good idea.

The two older women busy themselves in the kitchen.
JENNIFER *is left at the table.*

CHRISTINE: *(whispering)* Do you think it was Bill?

PATRICIA: *(whispering)* Could be.

CHRISTINE: Bill's always so cheerful.

PATRICIA: So was Ian.

CHRISTINE: That's true.

PATRICIA: Cheerful right up to the end. When he was with any of us.

CHRISTINE: Yeah.

PATRICIA: None of us saw it coming.

CHRISTINE: I know.

PATRICIA: So could just as easily be Bill.

CHRISTINE: Yeah.

JENNIFER: (*full volume*) I don't need anything to eat. Really.

CHRISTINE: That's all right, girl, once we make it it'll be here, then. In case you get hungry later.

JENNIFER: But—

CHRISTINE: Jenny. Pat's just going to make sandwiches now. Okay?

Beat.

JENNIFER: Okay.

Beat.

JENNIFER: I like turkey. If she has it.

PATRICIA *is fully absorbed in the making of sandwiches.*

CHRISTINE: (*coming back to the table*) So, Jenny. How are you finding the café?

Beat.

JENNIFER: Seriously?

CHRISTINE: What?

JENNIFER: We're going to have a chat about my summer job? Now?

CHRISTINE: What else would you like to talk about, Jenny?

JENNIFER: I . . . I don't know.

Pause. JENNIFER *glances at* PATRICIA, *but her head is down.*

JENNIFER: It's Jennifer. Or Jenn. Nobody calls me Jenny.

CHRISTINE: Okay.

Beat.

JENNIFER: It's all right. The scrubs-for-uniforms thing is a bit weird, but at least they're comfortable.

CHRISTINE: They're to make us look clean, Jennifer.

JENNIFER: Sure. I mean, I'll wear teddy bears and duckies anytime over those stupid brown visors at Tim Hortons.

CHRISTINE: You used to work at Tim Hortons?

JENNIFER: Yeah, Yonge and Carlton.

CHRISTINE: What's that?

JENNIFER: Uh, Toronto?

CHRISTINE: Right.

JENNIFER: It was super busy there. Everyone was stressed all the time. There was never a moment to breathe. I used to come off a whole shift and realize I never even had time to pee.

CHRISTINE: That's busy.

JENNIFER: Yeah and there were never enough people in the kitchen, so if you didn't have customers because of some miracle, you'd wind up helping out there. Doing dishes and stuff when you could have been getting a snack or just sitting down. Compared to that, the café here is a piece of cake. Even in the mornings when all the old men come in.

Beat.

JENNIFER: Aunt Mary hates that they stay so long, but I don't mind. They're funny.

CHRISTINE: That's cause all their jokes are new to you. Just you watch, they've only got another couple of days' worth.

JENNIFER: Are they in every day?

CHRISTINE: Unless there's a funeral.

A pause.

CHRISTINE: I suppose they needs a chance to talk to each other. Most of them are retired now, or they works up at the plant when it's on the go, but that's not a very conversational environment.

JENNIFER: Mmm.

Beat.

CHRISTINE: We needs a chance to chat with each other too, that's why we're all over here. Gives us a chance to check in, you know, make sure everyone is okay. Get out of the house once a week at least. We started because we had a . . . About a year ago there was a . . .

CHRISTINE glances toward the kitchen but PATRICIA is still very busy. CHRISTINE lowers her voice.

CHRISTINE: Well, Pat and Kathy lost their brother.

JENNIFER: Oh.

CHRISTINE: And we thought we probably shouldn't leave them alone to stare at the walls while their husbands were out at the café, so we piled in.

JENNIFER: Right. That's . . . well, good, I guess.

CHRISTINE: They weren't even talking to each other at the time. Sisters need each other in times like that, you know?

PATRICIA arrives at the table with a plate of sandwiches. She puts it down in front of JENNIFER.

JENNIFER: Thank you.

PATRICIA: *(to JENNIFER)* Ian shot himself.

CHRISTINE: Pat—

PATRICIA: You've started the story now, Chris, she might as well know the whole of it. *(To JENNIFER)* He was supposed to come up to my place for dinner but he never did, so I went over with a plate for him that afternoon and found—

The phone rings. PATRICIA answers.

PATRICIA: Yeah. Hi Gert.

There is a pause as she listens. CHRISTINE and JENNIFER are focused on the phone.

PATRICIA: Okay, thanks. Thanks for calling. Yeah.

She hangs up.

PATRICIA: Kevin.

The kettle goes off. PATRICIA *and* CHRISTINE *don't move to get it.*

Blackout. The whistle continues in the dark.

SCENE 2

Lights up on the kitchen, two hours later. JENNIFER *and* EUNICE *are at the table, peeling potatoes.* PATRICIA *is doing dishes.*

EUNICE: . . . so he comes in, larger than life, he's got his fancy silver computer and he's just roaming around town on foot, right? Just looking at things. Got really interested in the old shop down by the wharf that's been closed for . . . Jeez, Pat, how long has that old antique shop been closed?

PATRICIA: Oh, thirty years at least. Mom was alive.

EUNICE: Right, so thirty years, its clapboard is stripped right bare from the wind. Don't know why the town doesn't tear it down. Anyway, this youngster, he's right fascinated with this shop, right? He wants to go in, poke around, so he goes into the café to ask after it and Christine just charms him into staying for lunch. And then she goads him into having a slice of cheesecake. And I'm not saying that cheesecake isn't good, no, it's excellent, but he just dies for it. And he pops open that computer and he writes a whole article about how good the cheesecake is, and how charming Christine is, and wouldn't you know but it was in the next weekend's *Telegram*. I don't know if Kathy's got a copy around here. Pat?

PATRICIA: I wouldn't say.

EUNICE: I got one, it's on my fridge. I'll show you sometime.

JENNIFER: There's a copy framed at the café.

EUNICE: Oh yes, you're right, there is, too. Up by the counter. You read that next time you work, now. You can see we're all some proud of our Christine.

A pause. They peel potatoes. EUNICE *glances at* KATHY's *bedroom door.*

PATRICIA: Did he ever find out who owns that shop?

EUNICE: You know, I don't think he ever did. Isn't that funny.

Nobody laughs. Pause. They peel potatoes. CHRISTINE *comes in the side door with a giant pot. The lid is taped on with packing tape.*

CHRISTINE: Pat, can you help me with this?

PATRICIA *takes the pot from* CHRISTINE *and heaves it up onto the stove.* CHRISTINE *takes off her shoes and coat.*

PATRICIA: What's this?

CHRISTINE: Gert done up a pot of chili for Kathy. Says it's her favourite. We can bring 'er to a boil and she'll be ready right away. Good for lunch.

PATRICIA: I made sandwiches.

CHRISTINE: Soup and sandwiches, then.

PATRICIA: Yeah.

EUNICE: Minds you takes the tape off before you heats it, Patricia.

PATRICIA: Yeah.

PATRICIA begins to peel tape.

EUNICE: How's things down to the café?

CHRISTINE: Shut down. Gert sent all the men out, but they're only down to the wharf with their takeout cups now. All the rigs are still parked out front.

PATRICIA: Typical.

CHRISTINE: Mary called and said to close for the day. She wanted to come right back, too, but Stephen got an appointment to follow up about his hernia and you knows if they miss it it'll take at least a month before he can get back in. I told her we'd look out to Jenny till they were done.

JENNIFER: It's Jennifer.

CHRISTINE: Mm-hmm.

Beat.

JENNIFER: I don't need anyone to look after me.

EUNICE: Well, girl, there's no reason you can't go home to Mary's, is there?

JENNIFER: I left my keys at work.

EUNICE: Chris can bring you down to get them, right?

CHRISTINE: Now hang on, I made your Aunt Mary a promise. You're with us for the afternoon, like it or not.

JENNIFER: Great.

EUNICE: She'd only be next door, Chris.

CHRISTINE: Gert's gone home out of it now. And there's work to be done here.

Beat.

EUNICE: Well all right then, you're stayin'. We'll send you over at suppertime with a plate each for your aunt and uncle, to thank them for the chili.

JENNIFER: Gert made the chili.

EUNICE: It'll be Mary paid for the ingredients, though. Only fair.

CHRISTINE: Right.

PATRICIA: How much bloody Jesus tape did she use?

CHRISTINE: Looks like most of a roll, don't it. Here, girl, just cut it and have done.

EUNICE: The tape'll stink up the kitchen when you heat it.

CHRISTINE: We'll open a window.

PATRICIA: I don't know where she keeps the scissors.

CHRISTINE: Use a knife, Pat.

PATRICIA: Right.

PATRICIA *pulls a knife out of the dish rack, cuts the tape and plops the knife back down in the sink. Everyone watches her do it. She pulls off the lid and turns on the burner, a little shakily.*

PATRICIA: I, um, I've got to go put on lunch for the boys. Chris, you'll watch the pot?

EUNICE: They can fend for themselves, can't they, Pat, love?

PATRICIA: Not if I want to find my kitchen intact.

CHRISTINE: Why don't you just bring over some of these sandwiches?

PATRICIA: No, those are for Kathy. Will you watch the pot?

CHRISTINE: Yes, but—

PATRICIA: I'll be back the once.

CHRISTINE: All right.

The room is quiet while PATRICIA *puts on coat and boots and leaves. Once the door is closed:*

CHRISTINE: Well now.

EUNICE: That's something, isn't it?

CHRISTINE: It is, yeah.

JENNIFER: What is?

EUNICE: You got to set that stuff aside at a time like this.

CHRISTINE: That's right.

EUNICE: I only wish they'd tell us what the matter is. It's been months of this now. Breaks my heart.

JENNIFER: What are you talking about?

CHRISTINE: They're not getting along, I told you.

JENNIFER: Who?

CHRISTINE: (*gesturing to* KATHY's *room, then the side door*) Kathy and Patricia. Ever since their brother died. Neither of them will say why. There'll be times when they seem friendlier, but then they go right back to snipping at each other.

EUNICE: But today, well, Kath needs her sister, right?

CHRISTINE: She's just being selfish.

JENNIFER: She said she'd be back.

CHRISTINE: All I'll say is if Cameron can boil rice without burning down the house, I'm sure Pete can too. They won't go starving to death.

EUNICE: Sure the boys are probably up to Shieldstown anyway.

CHRISTINE: That's right, you know they're at McDonald's this very minute. Childish, that's what it is.

JENNIFER: Her brother-in-law just died.

EUNICE: Yes dear, and now her sister needs her.

JENNIFER: Sure but—

CHRISTINE: And she runs off home out of it like it's any old day.

JENNIFER: She probably needs some space for herself.

CHRISTINE: You got to be an only child. Sisters stick together, you'd know that if you had one. Or if your mother'd bothered to stick by her own family.

JENNIFER: You don't know anything about my mother.

CHRISTINE: I know more'n you think.

Beat.

CHRISTINE: How're you doing with those potatoes?

JENNIFER: I'm almost done.

CHRISTINE: Good, then, you can start on the parsnips.

CHRISTINE opens the fridge looking for parsnips.

EUNICE: I'll get them.

There is a pause while EUNICE crosses to the kitchen and fishes the parsnips out of a plastic grocery bag on the counter. She rinses them in the sink. CHRISTINE closes the fridge and opens several drawers.

EUNICE: What are you looking for?

CHRISTINE: Ladle.

EUNICE: Huh.

She looks around vaguely while rinsing. CHRISTINE continues to open and close drawers.

JENNIFER: It's right there. On the counter, I can see it from here.

CHRISTINE finds it in a cylinder of kitchen spoons and pulls it out, then stirs the chili.

CHRISTINE: This is almost ready, I think. Thank goodness for Gert.

EUNICE *drops the wet parsnips off with* JENNIFER, *then crosses to stand outside* KATHY's *bedroom.* CHRISTINE *pours out a bowl of chili.* EUNICE *taps gently on the door with a knuckle.*

EUNICE: Kathy?

Pause.

EUNICE: Kathy, there's lunch here. Are you hungry?

Beat.

EUNICE: Pat made some sandwiches, and Gert sent down some chili from the café.

KATHY (*off*): No. Thank you.

EUNICE: All right, love, it'll be here whenever you wants it.

There is a pause while they wait for a reply that never comes. CHRISTINE *puts the bowl of chili down next to the sandwiches.*

CHRISTINE: You want some chili, Jennifer?

JENNIFER: No, thanks.

JENNIFER *begins to peel parsnips.*

EUNICE: Chris, you got the meat on soak?

CHRISTINE: I have, yeah. Been in for about an hour.

EUNICE: You're a good hand.

CHRISTINE: I'd say I knows my way around a feed of Jiggs'. When Cameron's mother was alive I had to do one every Sunday.

EUNICE: Proper thing, we got to feed our old people.

CHRISTINE: Yes, but it had to be Jiggs' every week. I got awful sick of mashed turnip, I can tell you. Jenny, you ever had Jiggs' before?

JENNIFER: Jennifer, and yes, Mom does it every fall. She does a ham for Thanksgiving and then makes Jiggs' with the leftovers.

EUNICE: That's not real Jiggs' then.

JENNIFER: She says it's better for us because there's less salt. I don't even know if you can get salt meat in Toronto.

EUNICE: They got everything up there except the good stuff, that's what I say.

JENNIFER: I always hated it. Whole soggy carrots . . . what is that?

CHRISTINE: You hated it because she wasn't doing it right. You'll have a real feed now the once.

JENNIFER: And turnip greens are just about the worst of every green vegetable. Super bitter.

CHRISTINE: Now what's your mother doing raising you not to eat your greens?

JENNIFER: I eat them. I just don't like them.

EUNICE: Come on, now Chris, Amanda never liked the turnip greens neither. Or have you forgotten what it's like to have children?

CHRISTINE: Jeremy always ate his greens.

EUNICE: Because you made him.

CHRISTINE: Of course I made him. That's what parents do. We exist to cause our children pain and strife. Especially when they're teenagers. Right Jenny?

Pause.

JENNIFER: It's Jennifer.

Beat.

CHRISTINE: How're those parsnips, Jennifer?

JENNIFER: Fine, Christine. Am I doing the whole bag?

CHRISTINE: Yes, and when you're done I'll get you on a bag of carrots.

JENNIFER: What about the peels?

CHRISTINE: You can throw them out.

JENNIFER: Is there compost?

CHRISTINE: We don't have that here.

JENNIFER: Okay.

She gets up and passes CHRISTINE *to throw out the peels in the kitchen garbage. She returns to her place at the table, glancing at* KATHY'*s bedroom door as she sits down.*

EUNICE: You know, my mother used to squeeze every bit of life out of every piece of food. She'd boil down peelings and onion skins and chicken bones and everything in the biggest pot she had, and then she'd do it again. Nothing ever went to waste. It takes such a long time, though.

JENNIFER: It's fine.

CHRISTINE: You don't got to judge us for it.

JENNIFER: I'm not judging.

CHRISTINE: Yes I daresay.

JENNIFER: If you put vegetable peels in the garbage rather than the compost at home, they fine you.

EUNICE: Yes, b'y!

JENNIFER: Yes.

> *Beat.*

CHRISTINE: Well that's just money-grubbing from the city, isn't it?

EUNICE: That's right. Folks around here would never put up with it.

CHRISTINE: Can you imagine? Fined for putting out your garbage?

EUNICE: I'd say it's nobody's business but mine what I puts in my garbage, is it?

CHRISTINE: Indeed it isn't.

JENNIFER: I'm done with the parsnips.

EUNICE: Very good, girl, put them in a bowl, now. Hold on.

She looks through cupboards, finds a large bowl and brings it to the table. JENNIFER *puts the parsnips in it. At the same time,* CHRISTINE *gets the carrots out of the fridge and brings them over.*

CHRISTINE: Carrots.

JENNIFER takes them but does not look at CHRISTINE. *EUNICE sits down with her to help peel.*

EUNICE: So, Jennifer. I haven't seen your mother in a dog's age. Is this your first summer up home?

JENNIFER: The first whole one. Mom used to ship me out here for a few weeks every year when I was little.

EUNICE: I'd say your grandparents appreciated that.

JENNIFER: *(a little smile)* I think so, yeah. Probably almost as much as my parents did.

EUNICE: It's a good place for kids. Safe. Lots of room to play.

JENNIFER: I was always bored. None of my friends were here and there wasn't anything to do.

CHRISTINE: What are you doing back, then? We're not boring you?

JENNIFER: I'm not sure about university. But Mom says if I want to take a gap year I have to move out.

CHRISTINE: She kicked you out, then.

JENNIFER: No. Well, yeah, I guess. But like, only for the experience of living on my own.

CHRISTINE: With your relations, you mean.

EUNICE: Nothing wrong with staying with family.

JENNIFER: Toronto's so expensive, and when Aunt Mary offered the job I figured I could come and build up some cash.

EUNICE: And then what?

JENNIFER: I don't know.

CHRISTINE: Back to Toronto.

JENNIFER: I honestly don't know.

EUNICE: Your mother must miss you. It's good for kids to move out, of course, but I can't imagine sending my child out of the house, on purpose like that.

CHRISTINE: I remember her mother, and that's just like her. I'm surprised she even had a kid to begin with.

JENNIFER *doesn't know what to do with this.*

EUNICE: Chris—

CHRISTINE: So it's not your fault, I guess, considering who raised you. Good work on the carrots.

JENNIFER: What's your problem—

The bedroom door opens, and KATHY comes in. She is rather the worse for wear. A pause as everyone takes her in.

KATHY: Hello.

EUNICE: You want some lunch, Kathy?

KATHY: No.

EUNICE: You should eat something.

KATHY: Not hungry, Eunice, thanks.

Beat.

KATHY: *(to* JENNIFER*)* You're still here.

JENNIFER: *(indicating* CHRISTINE*)* She won't let me leave.

CHRISTINE: I promised Mary.

EUNICE: She's a good hand, Kath, she's got the vegetables almost ready to go in.

KATHY: You're making dinner? There's already/ too much food.

EUNICE: /We just want to set you up so you don't have to think about anything. We'll freeze that chili in batches and you can reheat it when you don't have the energy to make anything from scratch.

KATHY: Right.

EUNICE: And the Jiggs' is just to get you started.

Beat.

KATHY: We eat Jiggs' at Christmas.

EUNICE: It's no trouble. Jennifer's done a lot of the work.

JENNIFER *smiles weakly at* KATHY. *Pause.*

KATHY: I just came out for a drink.

EUNICE: I'll put the kettle on.

KATHY: Not tea.

KATHY *goes directly to the freezer and roots around in the back. She has to take items out to reach what she's looking for. She lays them on the counter.*

EUNICE: What are you looking for, Kath, can I—

KATHY: No, I've got it.

Finally she pulls out a bottle half-filled with whisky. She closes the freezer, gets a glass, and sits down at the table.

KATHY: Who wants a tipple?

CHRISTINE: No thank you.

EUNICE: I'm fine, love.

KATHY *pours herself a large swallow. Beat. She slides the bottle slowly over to where* JENNIFER *is sitting.*

KATHY: You want some?

JENNIFER: No thanks.

Beat. KATHY *considers* JENNIFER.

KATHY: You ever hear a shotgun go off before?

Beat.

JENNIFER: You mean before . . .

KATHY: Before today.

Beat.

JENNIFER: No.

KATHY: You want some whisky?

JENNIFER: Hell yes.

KATHY: Tumblers are first door on the right over the sink. There should be ice in the freezer if you want it.

> JENNIFER *gets a glass and some ice. She goes back to the table and takes a small pour.* EUNICE *puts the freezer foods back in the freezer.* JENNIFER *sits down and is about to taste it but:*

KATHY: Wait. A toast.

> *Everyone is quiet.*

KATHY: To Kevin.

JENNIFER: To Kevin.

> *They clink glasses and sip.* JENNIFER *hates the taste.*

KATHY: May God have mercy on his soul.

> KATHY *sips.*

EUNICE: Oh I'm sure—

KATHY: May He forgive his lying, evasive, self-destructive heart.

> *She sips.*

CHRISTINE: Kathy are you—

KATHY: May his mother forgive him for getting blood and bone and brains all over her nice new wallpaper.

She sips.

EUNICE: I don't—

KATHY: And when he gets to the pearly gates, I hope he's locked out overnight.

She finishes her drink and pours herself another one. Silence as KATHY *swirls her whisky.*

KATHY: Jennifer.

JENNIFER: Yes?

KATHY: Do you know where this whisky came from?

JENNIFER: No.

KATHY: It was a wedding present. (*She takes a sip.*) We opened it on our wedding night, and every year on our anniversary we would take a drink from it. Until the last couple of years.

JENNIFER: Oh. It's, um. It's good.

KATHY: It is, isn't it.

CHRISTINE: Are you sure you want to be drinking it now, Kathy?

KATHY: Why not? There's not going to be any more anniversaries.

CHRISTINE: Well, but . . .

Beat.

KATHY: But what, Christine? But it's the middle of the day?

CHRISTINE: That's . . . no, that's not . . .

A little beat.

EUNICE: She's thinking that you probably aren't clear-headed right now, and you might want to do something special with it once you've had a few days to think about it.

KATHY: What would I want to do that's special? I'd just be drinking it. There's other whisky in the world that I can drink when I've had a few days to think about it.

JENNIFER: But this was yours and Kevin's. Would he be all right with my having some?

KATHY: Fuck Kevin. Have your drink. Have another one after. He owes it to you. He ruined your day. (*Beat.*) He ruined my life. He ruined my whole life.

EUNICE: Kathy, don't you think you should have a lie-down?

KATHY: No. I'm going to have a drink. Since you are all here cooking me Christmas dinner, I suppose I don't need to be at anything else today, do I? It's happy hour.

She drinks.

KATHY: Where is my sister?

Beat. EUNICE *and* CHRISTINE *share a look.*

EUNICE: She just stepped out for—

JENNIFER: She went home to fix lunch for her husband and sons.

KATHY: Did she.

Silence.

JENNIFER: She said she'd be back.

KATHY: Hmm.

Beat.

KATHY: And what do you think about that, Jennifer?

JENNIFER: Uh . . .

KATHY: If your kid sister's husband shot himself, would you beat it home to take care of someone else?

Beat.

EUNICE: Now Kathy, I'm sure she's just making sure /they'll be all right while she comes to stay with you—

CHRISTINE: /She'll be back soon, that's what she said—

KATHY: Shhhhhhhh. (*Beat.*) I was asking Jennifer.

Beat.

JENNIFER: . . . I'm seventeen.

KATHY: And?

JENNIFER: I know how to make a sandwich.

KATHY: Ah. But you're a girl, Jennifer. Sandwiches are part of your womanly responsibility.

Beat.

KATHY: Couldn't ask a man to make a meal. He'll make a mess of it. And the kitchen.

JENNIFER: Well, that's bullshit.

CHRISTINE: Watch your language.

EUNICE: That's just how we were raised, that's all. A lot has changed recently on that front.

KATHY: Has it? Christine. You cook all day. Half the year you're the only one in the house who's working. When was the last time you came home and found your supper waiting for you?

Pause.

KATHY: This is not a rhetorical question, Christine. When was it?

CHRISTINE: Um. May. Mother's Day, before Jeremy was deployed.

KATHY: Right, you told us this. Jeremy cooked it?

CHRISTINE: Yeah.

KATHY: And what was it?

CHRISTINE: (*with a tickle of a giggle*) . . . Spaghetti. Soggy, overcooked spaghetti with canned tomato sauce.

EUNICE: It was good of him to try.

KATHY: (*matching the building need for laughter*) And for dessert?

CHRISTINE: . . . a slice of cheesecake he bought down to the café.

JENNIFER: You make the cheesecake at the café.

CHRISTINE: Yep.

JENNIFER: He bought you a slice of your own cheesecake for Mother's Day?

CHRISTINE *laughs, a bit madly.*

CHRISTINE: He did. And he got me butterscotch, too. I hate butterscotch.

The ladies laugh. EUNICE *is the least inclined to join in.*

KATHY: Have a drink, Christine.

CHRISTINE: Yes, all right.

As CHRISTINE *goes to the cupboard for a glass and pours herself some whisky:*

KATHY: I can't remember the last time I came home to find supper ready. If I was late Kevin would make something for himself and I'd find the dishes stacked in the sink. Or out on the table with the crumbs still on.

CHRISTINE: I can relate to that!

KATHY *and* CHRISTINE *clink glasses.*

JENNIFER: Dad does most of the cooking at home. Mom does the special occasion stuff, but Dad's home earlier so it's easier for him to do it.

EUNICE: Imagine.

KATHY: I think we were probably still dating the last time Kevin cooked for me. He used to do it all the time at first. Liked to show off that he knew how.

CHRISTINE: Cam doesn't do much beyond barbecuing. To be fair on him, though, I hate his cooking and don't mind telling him so!

Laughter. EUNICE *is increasingly uncomfortable.*

KATHY: Baby steps, hey, from when we were kids. If it weren't for Eunice we'd've actually starved to death after Mom passed.

EUNICE: It was my pleasure dear—

KATHY: Kevin used to mix up mustard and tomato sauce and put it on chicken. He called it "chicken cacciatore." And it wasn't even that bad, honestly.

JENNIFER: I've eaten worse than that.

CHRISTINE: Last Mother's Day I wouldn't have minded that cacciatore one bit.

JENNIFER *and* CHRISTINE *laugh.*

KATHY: Now, I happen to know firsthand that my nephews can make a mean bowl of Kraft Dinner. They even melt real cheese into it. Tablespoon of Cheez Whiz for good measure.

CHRISTINE: That's the good stuff.

KATHY: My sister's not raising her boys to be useless.

CHRISTINE: I'd say she isn't, smart woman like her.

KATHY: So it makes you wonder, doesn't it, why she'd run home this afternoon to feed them. Chris, you said Pete was at the café.

CHRISTINE: He was, yeah.

JENNIFER: He was still there when I left, too.

CHRISTINE: You know which one is Pete?

JENNIFER: Yeah, he always leaves a tip.

KATHY: So he was there when it happened. So he knows what's on the go.

CHRISTINE: Don't go flirting with Pete, Jennifer, no matter what kind of tip he leaves you.

JENNIFER: I don't flirt with him. I don't flirt with any of them.

CHRISTINE: Yes now.

KATHY: He wouldn't be expecting Pat home at all today, given the circumstances.

CHRISTINE: Then why is it that none of them can keep their tongues in their mouths when you're around?

JENNIFER: I don't know, Christine, I can't control what they do!

KATHY: You might even go out on a limb and say that he'd have texted the boys to let them know, too.

EUNICE: Yes, I'd say the boys know about their uncle by now.

CHRISTINE: Pete in particular, though, Jenny, leave him out. He's bad news for you.

Beat.

JENNIFER: What does that mean?

CHRISTINE: You don't know what's on the go around here and I'm trying to keep you from stepping in it.

KATHY: There's/ a reason—

JENNIFER: /You think I'd go for a guy like Pete? Married, got kids my age? Pete?

KATHY: He does have/ a history—

CHRISTINE: /You shouldn't tease them like that.

JENNIFER: Teasing, flirting . . . you mean smiling? Listening? Laughing when they're funny?

CHRISTINE: Exactly! God, you really are your/ mother's daughter—

JENNIFER: /That's not flirting, that's . . . that's being a good server. That's being a good person!

KATHY: (*finally breaking through*) Christine. What Jennifer here doesn't understand is that there's a reason Pat goes home every day to make him lunch.

A pause. CHRISTINE *and* EUNICE *share a realization.*

CHRISTINE: Oh, of course.

Beat.

JENNIFER: What?

KATHY: She wants to see if he's there.

CHRISTINE: She wants to remind him how good he got it.

EUNICE: She doesn't want anyone thinking it's her fault.

KATHY: There you go.

KATHY drinks. Pause.

JENNIFER: Does she know you talk about her like this?

KATHY: Oh, Jennifer. Not too many people around here who don't know what's going on there. Can't imagine she doesn't know everyone's talking about it.

CHRISTINE: Not after the way he and missus from up the shore got on at the Legion dance last month, anyway.

KATHY: Eunice, would you call down to Pat's? Jennifer's right, we shouldn't be telling tales behind her back. See if she'll come back over, would you?

EUNICE doesn't move.

KATHY: I'm serious, Eun, she should be here, and not waiting on that idiot she's married to hand and foot. Or don't you agree.

EUNICE goes to the phone and dials. Everyone is quiet while EUNICE is on the phone. CHRISTINE starts to tidy up around the kitchen, wiping down counters. KATHY drinks.

EUNICE: Patricia, love, it's Eunice . . . oh, yes, love, we're all here. Pat, Kathy's come out . . . . Yes, that's right, she's out of her room, dear . . . yes and she's asking after you . . . well, you're her sister, dear, she only wishes you were here . . . . Yes, all right my dear, we'll see you soon.

She hangs up.

EUNICE: Said she'll be right over.

KATHY: Good.

Pause. KATHY, *having finished her drink, pours herself another.*

KATHY: Anyone else?

EUNICE: No /thank you.

CHRISTINE: /None// for me.

JENNIFER: //No thanks.

KATHY: More for me, then.

She sips. Pause.

KATHY: Jennifer.

JENNIFER: Yes?

KATHY: Do you know what triage is?

JENNIFER: It's, um, when you first get to the emergency room. A counter with a nurse.

KATHY: That's . . . yeah, that's right, but before it was a counter it was a system. For figuring out who needs the most help. So, say we get a call to a really bad accident on the highway, like a bus rolled over or something, and a whole bunch of people are hurt, way more than we can deal with all at the same time. We'll check over everyone really fast and assign them a colour. You following?

JENNIFER: I think so.

EUNICE *joins* CHRISTINE*'s efforts to tidy up, even though there is little to do.*

KATHY: If you're a green, that means you're mostly fine. Like, maybe some glass from a windshield cut you a bit, but you're okay.

JENNIFER: So, like, the walking wounded?

KATHY: Yeah, they can usually walk. So then yellow, that's someone who's got a real problem, they're going to need attention, but they're not going to keel over right that second. Like, broken bones and concussions and things, right? And then there's the reds, and they're about to go over the edge. They're unconscious, or they're having a heart attack, or something. Those people have to get to the hospital right away. And in a crisis like that, you usually only have time to take care of the people in the red zone, and you, like, you keep an eye on the yellow people in case they flip over into red, and you pretty much ignore the folks in the green and black categories altogether.

JENNIFER: What's black?

KATHY: Huh? Oh. Black is dead. Or past saving.

Beat. EUNICE *and* CHRISTINE *stop tidying.*

KATHY: And you have to be decisive about what's red and what's black. Because you can't save everyone, right? And if you spend your time trying to save someone who can't be saved, then people who could live if you just paid attention to them . . . they'll go black themselves. And the yellows go red, and everything just goes to shit.

> *Beat.* KATHY *swirls her glass.* JENNIFER *doesn't know what to say, but* KATHY *is no longer speaking to her.*

KATHY: So you've got to do your triage right. Even if you know one of your patients in the black zone. Even if you love them.

> EUNICE *and* CHRISTINE *share a look.* KATHY *drinks deeply.*

> *Lights.*

SCENE 3

Lights up on the kitchen. The Jiggs' is on the stove alongside the chili. KATHY *sits at the table, finishing the last of the whisky.* EUNICE *and* CHRISTINE *also sit at the table with mugs of tea.* JENNIFER *is washing dishes with no particular urgency.*

Silence. EUNICE *and* CHRISTINE *exchange a look and then return their gaze to* KATHY. KATHY *does not react to this.*

Enter PATRICIA *through the side door, holding a casserole dish.*

PATRICIA: Hello.

KATHY: Was he home?

PATRICIA: Who?

EUNICE *and* CHRISTINE *exchange a look.*

EUNICE: Where have you been, dear?

PATRICIA: Making hashbrown casserole. I'd just started when you called. Would have been a waste not to make it.

KATHY: You said you'd be right over.

PATRICIA: Yes, right after . . . and now I'm here.

KATHY: So you are.

An uncomfortably long silence.

PATRICIA: Take this from me, would you, so I can take off my boots?

She hands the dish to JENNIFER, *who holds it exactly as she receives it, unsure of what to do next.* PATRICIA *takes off her boots, lines them up neatly by the door, removes her hat and gloves and hangs her coat, and then comes into the kitchen to take the dish again. She sets it down on the table amidst the sandwiches, chili, and Jiggs'-making detritus.*

PATRICIA: It's still warm.

KATHY: Excellent. More food.

PATRICIA: You love this recipe.

KATHY: Do I?

PATRICIA: You used to beg Mom to make it. On cold days.

KATHY: Ah. But I have grown up. On cold days now, I like to drink. Keeps me warm.

She snidely toasts her sister and finishes her drink. Pause.

CHRISTINE: I'd say your boys appreciate a good hashbrown casserole, don't they, Pat.

PATRICIA: Not like we used to.

KATHY: We used to have it with ketchup. Smother it in ketchup. It would be more ketchup than casserole.

PATRICIA: Ketchup soup with potatoes.

KATHY: And we'd get ketchup all over our mouths on purpose and pretend we were vampires out to suck each other's blood.

PATRICIA: I don't remember doing that.

KATHY: We did. We used to pick on Ian. Tell him we really were vampires and we were going to sneak into his room at night.

PATRICIA: Oh yeah. Huh.

KATHY: We used to scare him so bad he had to sleep in Mom's bed.

PATRICIA: That was you. I could never keep it up that long.

Beat.

EUNICE: You were only kids. Kids do things like that, it's normal.

KATHY: Yeah.

EUNICE: You were both lovely big sisters.

Beat.

KATHY: I need a drink.

CHRISTINE: You finished the bottle.

KATHY: That's okay. There's more in here somewhere. We just have to find it. Jennifer, are you up for a scavenger hunt?

JENNIFER: What do you mean?

KATHY: There are at least three bottles of something alcoholic hiding in this house.

JENNIFER: Uh . . . okay. Where?

KATHY: I don't know. That's why we have to *look* for them. Scavenger hunt, remember?

PATRICIA: You're not serious, Kathy.

JENNIFER: All right. (*She peels off her rubber gloves and starts looking around.*) I'll start with the cupboards?

KATHY: It would only be somewhere you wouldn't come across by accident.

JENNIFER: Where have you found them before?

KATHY: The back of top shelves. His sock drawer. Inside the toilet tank once.

PATRICIA: Jesus Christ.

KATHY: I did tell you, Patricia. Don't act so surprised.

JENNIFER *gets a chair and stands on it to look into the cabinets' top shelves.*

KATHY: Eunice. Would you be a dear and check the toilet?

EUNICE *hesitates.*

KATHY: Please. Just lift up the top of the tank.

EUNICE *goes off.*

JENNIFER: His drawers?

KATHY: I checked before I came out of the bedroom.

JENNIFER: Of course.

KATHY: You too, Christine, come on. Try in behind the baking pans.

CHRISTINE searches the lower cabinets.

EUNICE (*off*): Nothing!

KATHY: Check under the sink too!

EUNICE: All right, Kath, but I don't—oh—yeah. Hang on.

She emerges with a non-descript bottle.

EUNICE: Right in the back corner. Take a whiff, make sure it isn't bleach.

KATHY: Oh, trust me, this is not bleach.

CHRISTINE: This is honestly the weirdest thing we've ever done.

KATHY unscrews the cap and goes to swig directly, but thinks better of it and gives it a sniff. She makes a face.

KATHY: It's fucking coconut rum.

JENNIFER: Really? I actually *like* coconut rum.

KATHY: So did Kevin, but only when the boys weren't looking. And usually when he was already wasted. He must have been flying when he bought this.

JENNIFER: Two more?

KATHY: At least. Are you having fun?

Beat.

JENNIFER: A little bit.

KATHY: Good.

She pours some rum into her glass.

EUNICE: Are you sure you want to drink that, honey?

KATHY: Jesus, no. Coconut rum gives me flashbacks from high school. But someone's gotta drink the stuff and it might as well be the widow of the shining star who hid it under his bathroom sink.

Beat.

KATHY: I'm counting on you, Jennifer. Find a bottle of something else and I will trade you. I bet you're still too young to have a drink that triggers your gag reflex.

JENNIFER: Untrue. It's tequila for me.

JENNIFER has looked through all the upper cabinets and is onto the lower ones.

CHRISTINE: I'm looking down here.

JENNIFER: Well now so am I.

CHRISTINE takes items out of the cabinet and lays them on the counter as she searches, including the muffin box. KATHY brings her glass to her lips.

KATHY: Jesus, it smells like sour cough syrup.

CHRISTINE: Would you rather some more whisky?

EUNICE: Or how about a nice bottle of wine?

CHRISTINE: I can go over to Compton's and get you some.

KATHY: No. No wine. No buying alcohol when there's perfectly good booze in this house.

CHRISTINE: You just said—

KATHY: We are drinking Kevin's booze, all right? We are going to drink it until it's gone. We are systematically removing Kevin's secret, just-in-case alcohol from this house and we are going to have as much fun as possible while doing it.

She punctuates her point with a sip of the rum and chokes on it. She coughs and sputters.

KATHY: Even if it is like licking the inside of a rotten beach ball.

She takes another sip, a bit more successfully. A pause.

JENNIFER: Hold on. I got it!

KATHY: Where?

JENNIFER: Inside the toaster oven. Just a flask, though.

KATHY: The wily bastard. That's a piece of genius right there.

JENNIFER pours some out into her own glass.

JENNIFER: Rye. Trade?

KATHY: You knows.

They swap glasses, clink, and sip. KATHY enjoys the whisky thoroughly.

KATHY: I moved in with that toaster oven. I don't think we ever used it. Not once.

JENNIFER: We have one too that never gets used. We have a toaster, and we have an oven, so—

KATHY: Kevin always complained it took up too much space. I wouldn't get rid of it, though. Serves me right.

She drinks. Beat.

EUNICE: No, it doesn't.

KATHY: You don't know, so don't talk.

Pause.

EUNICE: Well. If you young ladies are going to be drinking, I think I'll put the kettle on. Tea, Christine?

CHRISTINE: Sure.

EUNICE: Patricia?

PATRICIA: No.

EUNICE: All right. For two.

EUNICE fills the kettle and puts it on the stove.

KATHY: (*to JENNIFER and the room at large*) When you put a kettle on a burner, do you know what happens? It heats the water at the bottom. But then the water that's warmer—heat rises, right, and it floats up to the top and new, cold water drops down toward the burner to get heated up. So, inside the kettle, there's a current—hot water up, cold water down—and there's no resisting it, it's just . . . it's just physics. And as the temperature rises the water takes up more and more space. And then it turns to steam, and it gets hotter and hotter and it expands so the pressure inside the kettle builds up until, finally, the steam has to escape, so it screams out through that tiny little hole because that's the only way out. And then we take this . . . traumatized water. We take it and we soak dead leaves in it, and we say there's nothing a good cup of tea can't fix.

> EUNICE *opens her mouth to say something, then thinks better of it and pulls two mugs out of the cupboard. She finds the muffin box on the counter and takes it to the garbage.* PATRICIA *clocks this and laughs.*

PATRICIA: You bought the muffins.

CHRISTINE: What?

PATRICIA: I knew it. They were store-bought muffins.

CHRISTINE: It doesn't matter, Pat—

PATRICIA: You accepted compliments on the muffins.

EUNICE: Pat, it isn't the time to—

PATRICIA: That's disappointing. I'm disappointed. Eunice, aren't you disappointed?

KATHY: Jennifer, have you ever seen a more supportive sister?

PATRICIA: Why in God's name would you lie about muffins?

KATHY: You know why. Actually. You do.

Everyone waits, but no explanation is forthcoming.
KATHY and PATRICIA face off. Pause. EUNICE goes to the
stove and gives the Jiggs' a stir.

EUNICE: Chris, I think she might be almost ready.

CHRISTINE: Oh yeah?

She joins EUNICE in the kitchen.

KATHY: (*sarcastic*) Excellent. Jiggs' dinner.

JENNIFER: Soggy, slimy vegetables. Delightful.

KATHY: Local delicacy.

JENNIFER: In France they eat snails, and those are basically snot. They have the taste and texture of snot, anyway. But at least you can chew them.

KATHY: And we eat it at Christmas. And funerals.

JENNIFER: Seems out of date. Like men who can't make their own sandwich.

   PATRICIA takes note of this, but says nothing. CHRISTINE
   clocks the dig.

CHRISTINE: Would you stay out of it? Just stay out of it, Jenny.

JENNIFER: It's Jennifer.

CHRISTINE: You got some nerve coming in here and looking down your nose at us. Going on about composting and soggy carrots and taking up space in this poor woman's kitchen.

JENNIFER: You made me stay—

CHRISTINE: You and your mother are the same, you know. Heed/less. Selfish.

JENNIFER: /Leave my mother out of it!

CHRISTINE: Taking up shifts from us who depend on that job. Less paid time this summer than the rest of the year, so far.

JENNIFER: It's not my fault you—

CHRISTINE: Wouldn't mind so much if it were one of the young people from around here. Maybe even your Amanda, Eunice. She could come home.

JENNIFER: Are you seriously blaming me for stealing your job? /Really? This is an immigration issue?

EUNICE: /Amanda wouldn't come home for a job at a café, Chris.

CHRISTINE: Jobs around here are scarce enough to begin with, let alone the ones you can enjoy. Kathy here is one of the lucky ones.

A short, humourless laugh from KATHY. *Silence. All eyes on* CHRISTINE, *whose eyes are on* KATHY. KATHY *drinks and looks at no one.*

CHRISTINE: Sorry, Kathy. Jesus I'm sorry I didn't mean to say—

KATHY: Yup.

She drinks again. Pause.

JENNIFER: This is about the men, isn't it? At the café?

KATHY: /Yes.

CHRISTINE: /No it's—

JENNIFER: All those men who come in every morning and normally chat and joke with you, but now they're coming to chat and joke with me. I've heard you and Gert making fun. Didn't know it upset you so much. One of those men is your husband, isn't he?

KATHY: She's onto you, Chris.

JENNIFER: Is he the one who always squeezes my elbow when I hand him his change? Or the one who always draws a winky face on the back of his bill? How flirty *is* your husband, on a scale of one to Pete?

A pause.

PATRICIA: I'm sorry, what?

JENNIFER: Oh don't worry, Patricia. Christine has warned me about Pete.

CHRISTINE: You shut your face.

JENNIFER: She warned me to stay away from your husband. Thinks he might try something.

PATRICIA: Ah.

Beat. PATRICIA *gets up.*

KATHY: Oh good, she's leaving again.

EUNICE: Pat, Chris was only looking out for—

KATHY: Run away, Pat. It's all about you today.

CHRISTINE: I didn't tell her anything you didn't know, Pat.

Pause.

PATRICIA: So you told her that he cheats on me.

JENNIFER: And she obviously thinks he might do it again.

CHRISTINE: You shut up.

PATRICIA: She knows my husband cheats. Like, not once, not a one-time slip up, but generally. Thanks, Chris, that's very helpful. I'm going.

KATHY: You should be leaving *him*, not me.

PATRICIA: Katherine, we are not going to talk about this now—

KATHY: Then when, Patricia? When, exactly, *is* the time? I've been saying this to you for . . . how long? At least five years. Pat. He cheats. He takes you for granted. He takes advantage of you. And every time he (*air quotes*) "slips up" you fucking *reward* him by being extra attentive. Have some goddamn self-respect.

PATRICIA: I made a promise. I promised to stay and work it out.

KATHY: He made the same promise! What the hell kind of effort has he put into "working it out"? Flirting with the child working at the café, apparently.

PATRICIA: You're upset right now—

KATHY: Don't tell me how I feel. We're talking about you and your asshole husband.

PATRICIA: Why can't you just stay out of it? Why can't all of you just stay out of it? Promises mean something to us. He hasn't left either, in case you didn't notice.

KATHY: He hasn't *left* because he has no reason to go. You wait on him hand and foot, and he can do literally whatever he wants because you let him.

EUNICE: Girls, I wonder if maybe now might not be the best time . . . for this . . . conversation.

PATRICIA: You're right, /Eunice.

KATHY: /Why, because my husband is dead, I can't express an opinion on my brother-in-law? When you go home, Patricia, why don't you ask Pete how recently he got Kevin drunk? Was it last night?

PATRICIA: I don't think /he meant to get—

KATHY: /I don't have to *think*, Pat, I *know* they go out together. That was your doing, as I remember. And when it got /out of hand, Pete wouldn't take it seriously.

PATRICIA: /You asked me to send them out together. You wanted them to be friends!

KATHY: Patricia!

PATRICIA: What?

KATHY: I couldn't get Pete to take Kevin's drinking seriously.

Pause.

PATRICIA: We didn't really have a handle on it, Kathy. *I* didn't, until this afternoon.

KATHY: I told you/about this!

PATRICIA: /You said you thought he was drinking too much, but so does Pete. So does everybody. If you ask anybody who works up to the hospital the whole G-D town is alcoholic.

KATHY: Not you. You don't like the taste. Or, possibly, you just say that to avoid offending people. Because you remember what it was like to live with Dad.

PATRICIA: Kevin was still getting to work every day. Taking care of himself. Or it looked like he was. It didn't seem . . . serious.

KATHY: Oh.

Beat.

KATHY: And if it did "seem serious," would you have understood me leaving?

Beat.

CHRISTINE: Kathy . . .

EUNICE: Leaving . . .?

PATRICIA: Katherine has been living in a hotel in Shieldstown for a month now.

KATHY: That's why I didn't bake my own fucking muffins. And don't tell me you didn't have an inkling.

CHRISTINE: We knew Kevin was stressed, but—

EUNICE: He loved you so much, honey.

CHRISTINE: We figured it would blow over.

KATHY: But not Patricia. She knew everything. Not that she was any kind of support.

EUNICE: You really moved out? Of this house?

CHRISTINE: And you didn't tell us?

EUNICE: Kath, we honestly had no idea. We could've—

CHRISTINE: Why didn't you say anything?

A pause.

JENNIFER: Oh my God. You actually don't get this.

Everyone looks at JENNIFER.

JENNIFER: She knew you would *judge* her! Talk about her behind her back. Like you've already been doing. Like you've been talking about my mother who you haven't even seen in twenty years, and about Patricia and her cheating husband, and about their brother who—

PATRICIA: You shut your goddamn face about my brother.

KATHY: She's more or less hit the nail on the head, though, Pat, hasn't she. You know we talk about you, right?

PATRICIA: Of course I do.

KATHY: You would have kept Pete's affairs a secret forever if you could've.

PATRICIA: I don't dump my personal business into everyone else's backyard.

KATHY: You didn't even tell your sister the first time.

PATRICIA: You would've hated him. I didn't want that.

KATHY: I do hate him. Doesn't seem to do any good, though.

PATRICIA: You hating him just makes it harder to get past it!

KATHY: If he wanted to get past it, he'd probably stop picking up women at dances. And coffee shops.

PATRICIA: Well, that isn't my fault.

KATHY: Leave him.

PATRICIA: I can't, and you know it.

KATHY: You can, though. It's not actually very complicated. I'll draw you a map—

PATRICIA: Katherine, I swore to God and under heaven and I am going to keep that promise until death does us part.

KATHY: Well. Death hath now parted me and Kevin. So I guess that simplifies the paperwork.

Beat. KATHY *is very near tears. She drinks again.*

PATRICIA: Kathy.

KATHY: You are never there when I need you. Not when I moved out. /Not now.

PATRICIA: /Kevin was good to you.

KATHY: Kevin was self-destructing.

PATRICIA: I thought you could stop him.

KATHY: I couldn't make him do anything. I asked him to talk to me about his stress and he wouldn't. I asked him to see a doctor about it and he wouldn't. I asked him to stop drinking so much and he just started lying to me about it.

PATRICIA: He was sick.

KATHY: I *know* he was sick, I deal with sick people every day of my life! Don't tell me what my husband was, I was married to him! I had to watch him drink himself unconscious in order to escape. Himself. His life. Me. And all my sister had to say about it was that I had a duty to stand by. My responsibility was to stay here and watch him implode!

PATRICIA: He loved you. He treated you well. He didn't cheat, or vanish for a week at a time with no notice. You showed up the day after our baby brother's funeral to cry your eyes out about your perfectly-fine marriage to your perfectly-nice husband and I was having nightmares about finding Ian all night long.

KATHY: It was *about* Ian. They're connected.

PATRICIA: What are you talking about?

KATHY: Ian. Dying. Killing himself. Kevin, killing himself. I was— grieving, obviously. And I saw it coming in Kevin and I was scared and upset, and you said I had to stick it out. That it was my job. You put it on me.

PATRICIA: I didn't—

KATHY: So now it's my fault, get it? It's my fault he imploded. It's my fault he died.

PATRICIA: It isn't—

KATHY: It was *my job* to save him, somehow, even though I knew I couldn't. You said it was. Maybe I should have called the police when he first bought the gun. Or the first time he pulled it out of the shed while he was wasted. Maybe if I'd reported it to someone he would've . . . would've gotten . . .

She gives up. Beat.

EUNICE: It's not your fault, Kathy.

KATHY: I know that! I fucking *know* that, it's *his* stupid fault. He's the one who was hiding from everyone, he's the one who *decided* to shoot himself. It's his fault.

Pause.

JENNIFER: Not just him. Or you. It's like, all of this.

CHRISTINE: Go home, Jennifer.

KATHY: No, she's right. In a vacuum, he'd be alive. It's this fucking place. He was hiding it, and I was hiding it, and when it all fell apart between us, we both hid it. We cut ourselves off from everyone. And you're hiding it, too, Pat, you're trying to hide the shit in your marriage, and Ian was hiding his shit from us. From us, his family, every time he smiled when he didn't mean it. /Jesus Christ, Pat—

PATRICIA: /He was always smiling, Kathy—

KATHY: —do you remember what he used to look like when he was smiling and he meant it? I got so used to the fake smile I can't remember the last time our kid brother was actually happy. But we *made* him fake it, /we teased him for not smiling—

PATRICIA: /I never did that—

KATHY: —we gave him a hard time for spending too much time in the basement, we *made* him pretend. / Turns out pretending too hard can be fatal.

PATRICIA: /Kathy. Stop it. Don't you think I kick myself every day for not noticing there was something wrong? Don't you think I stay up nights running things I could've done differently over and over?

KATHY: Like what? What would you have done differently?

PATRICIA: I don't know . . . I would've. I would've brought him to you, probably.

KATHY: Right, because I am an expert in making someone not kill himself.

PATRICIA: You know about that stuff and I guess I thought—

KATHY: You thought you'd take him to the hospital. To see someone. To talk it out. Right? You thought maybe you'd bring your kid brother in for a chat and that might retroactively save his life.

PATRICIA: I didn't say it made sense, Kathy, /it's like a recurring nightmare.

KATHY: /So what were you going to do if he refused to go? If he didn't want to be seen needing to talk to someone about what was happening in his head?

PATRICIA: . . . I'd have told him that's ridiculous.

KATHY: Yeah. I tried that. Didn't go over.

Beat.

PATRICIA: Ian never told me you—

JENNIFER: She's not talking about Ian—

EUNICE: Jennifer.

KATHY: Why the *fuck* is it our job to take care of them if they can't be cared for? What's the point of that?

PATRICIA: I think Ian could have been cared for. If we knew.

KATHY: Oh. You do. So, do you feel guilty? Huh? Do you, big sister?

PATRICIA: Every day.

KATHY: Good. You should. You should have noticed what was going on. You should have helped him. Dragged him in to the doctor. Locked him in the car and driven him to a therapist in St. John's. Forced him to get better. You were his big sister. Our mother's gone. It was your job to take care of him, Patricia!

CHRISTINE: You're out of line, Kathy.

KATHY: I'm right, though, aren't I? (*to* PATRICIA) You know I am. That's why you can't sleep. That's why you dropped off the map after, even though I needed you. Maybe that's why you're working so hard to keep your toxic marriage alive. You're giving Pete the CPR that you should've given our brother!

PATRICIA: *Shame on you!* Feeling guilty doesn't make me guilty.

KATHY: Who else was supposed to notice?

PATRICIA: Where were you? /He was your brother too!

KATHY: /I had *Kevin!* Remember Kevin, I was married to him //until this morning, when—

PATRICIA: //I'm married too, Katherine, and it's not all roses!

KATHY: No *shit.* But *your* fella's not drinking himself into a stupor and then taking the rifle out of the shed and just staring at it like he's praying to it or something. Or is he? I wouldn't know, because apparently we have no idea how to talk about anything that matters! Tell me, Patricia, does he keep his gun in your shed at home or is it stashed at some other woman's place?

PATRICIA: Fuck you.

KATHY: Get out of my house.

CHRISTINE: Kath, she didn't mean—

KATHY: I know what she fucking meant. Leave.

EUNICE: Kathy—

KATHY: You too. All of you. Get out.

JENNIFER: I don't have—

KATHY: *Out!*

> *The ladies scramble to get coats/purses and leave with them dangling from their arms. During this:*

EUNICE: We'll call you later, all right, dear?

KATHY: I don't care.

CHRISTINE: You know where to find us/ when you come around.

KATHY: /Oh my God, please get out of my fucking house right fucking now.

They go. Once the door is closed, we hear them get into cars, drive away out of earshot. A long silence.

KATHY yanks the cord out of the phone and goes to the table. She takes it all in—the sandwiches, chili, casserole, peeled vegetables, et cetera—and then she flips it. The food goes everywhere. Pause.

There is something duct-taped to the underside of the table. KATHY pulls it free and finds that it's a flask of clear liquid. She sits down on the floor in the middle of the mess, holding it.

KATHY: Jesus Christ, Kevin. What the hell did you do.

Pause.

KEVIN enters from the bedroom. He is wearing his work clothes, fresh, as if he is just about to leave for the day.

KATHY watches him from the floor. He crosses to the kitchen.

KEVIN: Is there any roast left?

He opens the fridge. Beat.

KEVIN: Kath?

KATHY: Huh?

KEVIN: Is there roast left?

KATHY: I made you a box of leftovers. It's on the middle shelf.

KEVIN: Where? I don't see it.

KATHY: On the right, with the red lid.

KEVIN: It's not there, Kath.

KATHY: Oh my God. It's just—literally right there.

He feels around inside the fridge.

KATHY: No, down. The *middle* shelf. There.

He finds it.

KATHY: Why do you even have eyes if you can't look for things?

KEVIN *closes the fridge door.*

KEVIN: So I can see you give me looks like that one. (*He smiles at her.*) I'm gonna be late.

He crosses to the side door.

KATHY: Kevin?

KEVIN: Yeah?

KATHY: Happy anniversary.

Beat.

KEVIN: It always is.

KEVIN exits.

Lights change. It is now sunset. KATHY *hasn't moved. Silence. Then, a knock at the side door.* KATHY *does not answer.*

PATRICIA comes in. She stops just inside. A pause while she takes in the mess. KATHY *watches her.*

PATRICIA: Hi.

Beat.

KATHY: Hi.

Pause.

PATRICIA: I left my purse.

KATHY: Oh.

They do not move. Pause.

PATRICIA: Do you want help with . . .

She indicates the overturned table.

KATHY: No. Leave it.

Beat.

PATRICIA: All right.

Beat.

KATHY: It's honest.

Beat.

PATRICIA: Yeah.

Pause.

KATHY: Do you . . . Do you want a cup of tea?

Beat.

PATRICIA: Sure.

KATHY *doesn't move. Silence. Then:*

KATHY: Kevin's room. At his parents'? His old room. It was so clean. It smelled like lemons. Spotless. Except for . . . um, you know.

PATRICIA: Yeah. I do.

Beat.

KATHY: I don't think I . . . really thought about what it would look like in there. Ian's room. Before today.

PATRICIA: Why would you? If you could avoid it. It's . . . not something that's easy to get rid of.

KATHY: I guess not.

A long pause. PATRICIA *sits down on the floor with* KATHY, *in the middle of the mess.*

KATHY: I would offer milk and sugar but . . .

Both women take a glance at the overturned table.

PATRICIA: That's okay. We'll drink it black.

KATHY: Okay.

Silence.

KATHY: You know something? I was coming back. This morning, I decided. I woke up in my shitty motel room and I decided that being with him was worth it. I was going to come home and tell him that I wanted to move back in. I was going to try again. (*Beat.*) I thought there was still time.

Pause.

PATRICIA: It's not your fault.

KATHY: Isn't it?

Pause.

KATHY: I wish . . .

She scans the room with her eyes, the overturned table and associated mess. Her gaze lands on the side door. PATRICIA *watches her. Finally:*

PATRICIA: Me too.

Pause. Lights down.

SHARON KING-CAMPBELL is a theatre and literary artist based in Ktaqmkuk, colonially known as Newfoundland. She was the 2017 recipient of the Rhonda Payne Award, was longlisted for the CBC Poetry Prize in 2020, and is a four-time winner of the Arts and Letters Awards in fiction, dramatic script, and poetry. Her collection of poetry, *This is How It is*, was published in 2021. Her plays *Original* and *Give Me Back* have reached audiences throughout Newfoundland and Labrador and mainland Canada.